Dear Parents and Educators,

Welcome to Penguin Young Readers! As pare
know that each child develops at his or her ov
speech, critical thinking, and, of course, reac
Readers recognizes this fact. As a result, eacl
book is assigned a traditional easy-to-read level (1–4) as well as a
Guided Reading Level (A–P). Both of these systems will help you choose
the right book for your child. Please refer to the back of each book
for specific leveling information. Penguin Young Readers features
esteemed authors and illustrators, stories about favorite characters,
fascinating nonfiction, and more!

D0790665

Strawberry Shortcake™ Camp Berry	LEVEL **2**
	GUIDED READING LEVEL **G**

This book is perfect for a **Progressing Reader** who:
• can figure out unknown words by using picture and context clues;
• can recognize beginning, middle, and ending sounds;
• can make and confirm predictions about what will happen in the text; and
• can distinguish between fiction and nonfiction.

Here are some **activities** you can do during and after reading this book:
• Make Connections: In this story, Raspberry Torte helps nurse a hurt baby
  bird back to health. Have you ever cared for an animal that was hurt?
  Write a paragraph explaining how you helped the animal. If you haven't
  cared for one, use Raspberry's example to help explain how you would
  care for a hurt animal.
• Retelling: Retell the story of Strawberry Shortcake and her friends' time at
  Camp Berry. Use your berry fun voice and make sure not to leave out any
  important details!

Remember, sharing the love of reading with a child is the best gift
you can give!

—Bonnie Bader, EdM
Penguin Young Readers program

*Penguin Young Readers are leveled by independent reviewers applying the standards developed by Irene Fountas and Gay Su Pinnell in *Matching Books to Readers: Using Leveled Books in Guided Reading*, Heinemann, 1999.

To my own happy campers:
Danny, Josh and Sammi—MM

PENGUIN YOUNG READERS
Published by the Penguin Group
Penguin Group (USA) LLC, 375 Hudson Street, New York, New York 10014, USA

USA | Canada | UK | Ireland | Australia | New Zealand | India | South Africa | China

penguin.com
A Penguin Random House Company

ISBN 978-0-448-48153-1   10 9 8 7 6 5 4 3 2 1

PENGUIN YOUNG READERS
LEVEL 2
PROGRESSING READER

Strawberry Shortcake

Camp Berry

by Mickie Matheis
illustrated by Laura Thomas

Penguin Young Readers
An Imprint of Penguin Group (USA) LLC

Strawberry Shortcake is

in her café.

Plum Pudding runs inside.

She has big news.

Mr. Longface is starting

a summer camp.

There will be swimming, hiking,

crafts, and more.

Summer camp sounds berry fun!

Everyone wants to go.

The girls are excited

when the big day arrives.

First Mr. Longface takes them

to the lake.

He teaches the girls how to swim.

Plum Pudding swims to the dock.

Splash, splash, splash!

Mr. Longface gives Plum

a berry patch.

It is a special award.

The award is because Plum was
best at swimming.
Great job, Plum!

Next the girls learn

to paddle canoes.

Orange Blossom paddles

the farthest.

Mr. Longface gives her

a berry patch.

Good work, Orange!

The campers go to a picnic table.

It is covered with flowers

and twigs.

They make pretty crafts.

Lemon Meringue makes a crown

of flowers for her hair.

Pink, yellow, purple, and white!

The girls like Lemon's crown.

How beautiful!

Mr. Longface gives Lemon

a berry patch.

Well done, Lemon!

It is time for an archery lesson.

The girls take turns with the bow

and arrows.

Ready, aim, fire!

Cherry Jam hits the target.

Nice shot, Cherry!

She gets a berry patch.

Blueberry Muffin gets

a berry patch for building

the best campfire.

Good work, Blueberry!

Strawberry gets one for toasting

the perfect marshmallow.

Looks yummy, Strawberry!

At the end of the day,

the girls take a hike.

Mr. Longface leads the way.

Birds chirp.

Butterflies fly from

flower to flower.

Nature is fun!

But something is wrong.

Oh no!

Raspberry Torte is missing.

Where is Raspberry?

There she is!

Raspberry has found a baby bird.

The bird fell from its nest.

The baby bird needs help.

Raspberry picks up the bird.

Everyone walks back to camp.

Raspberry gives water to the bird.

Mr. Longface helps her bandage

its wing.

Time for a nap!

Raspberry stays with the bird.

After a nap,

the bird feels much better.

He is ready to fly home.

The campers wave good-bye
to the bird.

Now Mr. Longface has something
for Raspberry.

It is a berry patch!

She got it for helping the bird.

This makes Raspberry very happy.

Thank you, Mr. Longface!

Camp Berry was so much fun!

The girls cannot wait to go to

camp next summer!